Fairy SCHOOL Dropout

Undercover

BY

MEREDITH BADGER

WITHDRAWN

NOT FOR RESALE

SQUARE
FISH

Unless proceeds benefit the
City and County of San Francisco

Feiwel and Friends

New York

SQUARE FISH

An Imprint of Macmillan

FAIRY SCHOOL DROPOUT UNDERCOVER. Text copyright © 2007 by
Meredith Badger. Illustration and design copyright © 2007 by
Hardie Grant Egmont. All rights reserved. Printed in June 2011 in the
United States of America by R. R. Donnelley & Sons Company,
Harrisonburg, Virginia. For information, address Square Fish,
175 Fifth Avenue, New York, NY 10010.

Square Fish and the Square Fish logo are trademarks of Macmillan and
are used by Feiwel and Friends under license from Macmillan.

Library of Congress Cataloging-in-Publication Data
Badger, Meredith.
Fairy school undercover / by Meredith Badger.
p. cm. — (Fairy school dropout)
Summary: Having been expelled from three fairy academies, Elly relishes the
opportunity to attend a human school but she soon learns that it is not easy to pass as
a human being—even in a school with a Fairy Club.
ISBN 978-0-312-61951-0
[1. Fairies—Fiction. 2. Magic—Fiction. 3. Schools—Fiction.
4. Popularity—Fiction. 5. Clubs—Fiction.] I. Title.
PZ7.B1382Fak 2009
[Fic]—dc22
2008034761

First published in Australia by Hardie Grant Egmont
Originally published in the United States by Feiwel and Friends
First Square Fish Edition: July 2011
Square Fish logo designed by Filomena Tuosto
Illustrations by Michelle Mackintosh
Text design by Sonia Dixon Design
mackids.com

10 9 8 7 6 5 4 3 2 1

AR: 4.3 / LEXILE: 640L

31223095840279

FAIRY
SCHOOL
Dropout

Undercover

Chapter One

Everyone knows what fairies are. They are sweet, little creatures that live under toadstools. They dress in pink and they flutter around, making humans happy by granting wishes. And they know how to make magic from the day they are born. Right?

Wrong.

Look at this picture:

Can you tell which is the human and which is the fairy? Difficult, isn't it? Especially because the fairy (that's her on the right, by the way) has her wings safely tucked away beneath her clothes.

Let's get one thing straight: Not all fairies live in Fairydom. You might live next door to a fairy. There's probably one at your school. In fact, your best friend might be a fairy. Does she have no more than ten freckles? Is her hair always shiny? Do her fingers shimmer, ever so slightly, when she wiggles them?

These are all telltale signs of being a fairy. But don't bother asking her. She'll deny it. Fairies aren't allowed to reveal their true identities to humans, even to their best friends. Imagine if a kid knew they were friends with a fairy. They'd be asking for

favors *all* the time:

"Can you make my bike fly?"

"Can you turn my ham and cheese sandwich into a chocolate sprinkles one?"

"Can you make it Saturday forever?"

Which is why Elly Knottleweed-Eversprightly of 27 Raspberry Drive is so lucky to have a friend like Jess Chester. Jess couldn't care less about fairies and magic. She'd rather solve a problem herself than hope a fairy will come and fix it for her. This is lucky for Elly because Jess knows a secret about Elly.

A *big* secret.

Elly Knottleweed-Eversprightly is a fairy. She even has the wings to prove it. But Elly isn't a typical fairy. She hates pink, for one thing. She also hates flying and thinks her

skateboard is a much better way to get around. Elly and her family don't live under a toadstool, either. They live right next door to Jess and her family in an ordinary street in an ordinary town.

As for being *born* knowing magic, this only happens in rare cases. Unfortunately for Elly, one of these rare cases happens to be her baby sister, Kara. Imagine a toddler who can magically move things around, and turn them into other things! It can get very messy. For most fairies, though, magic is taught to them at a fairy school. This is where they go to learn spelling and extreme flying and all the other things fairies need to learn before they can earn their fairy license.

This probably sounds like lots of fun, and indeed, most fairies love school. They love

wearing fluffy pink dresses and carrying sparkling wands. They love learning how to loop-the-loop in midair. But Elly, as we've noted, is no typical fairy. She hates going to fairy school. Every time she goes to a new fairy school, it ends in disaster. And she's been to quite a few. Four, in fact.

But this term, everything was going to change. Elly was going undercover—at Jess's human school! No spells. No flying instruction. Just nice, normal, human stuff. Elly couldn't wait.

But Elly's undercover operation almost didn't happen. On the Sunday morning before Elly was to start at South Street School, Elly woke up and knew something was wrong. She lay there for a moment, trying to work out what it was. Did she get into trouble

yesterday? Had she fallen out of bed again? (It's never nice falling out of bed, but it's *particularly* bad when you're a fairy and your bed hovers six feet above the ground.)

But then she realized that it was a sound coming from her parents' room that was making her nervous. It was the sound of a suitcase being packed.

Elly jumped up and rushed into her mom and dad's room. Sure enough, there were her parents, busily throwing clothes at their self-packing suitcases, called Self-Packers.

"Elly! I'm glad you're up," said Elly's mom. She looked frazzled. Her hair was poking out at strange angles from her head and her shirt was on backward.

"Our plans have changed all of a sudden. I have to leave immediately on a work trip

with Kara and your dad."

Mrs. Knottleweed-Eversprightly is an inventor at the famous Fairy Inc. corporation. Fairy Inc. designs most of the gadgets that fairies use in their daily lives. The Self-Packers, for instance, were designed by Elly's mom. They're meant to make packing quicker. You just throw your clothes at the suitcase and it catches them in a mechanical arm, folds them, and places them neatly inside itself. The only problem is that Self-Packers are very fussy about what you pack. They don't like clothes that have holes in them, for one thing—even buttonholes.

As fast as Mr. and Mrs. Knottleweed-Eversprightly threw clothes at the suitcases, the mechanical arm of the Self-Packer would throw them back out again. It was making

packing a very long task, indeed.

Elly noticed that one suitcase was still on top of the wardrobe. Her suitcase.

"What about me?" she asked.

Her mother looked worried. "Unfortunately, you're not allowed to come. It's a top secret project."

This was a shock. Elly had never been left behind before. She had a horrible feeling she might cry. "I won't tell anyone," she said, blinking a lot. "I promise."

Mrs. Knottleweed-Eversprightly sighed. "I'm sorry, Elly. It's against the rules."

"So where will I go?" asked Elly.

Her parents looked at each other. "We were hoping that you could stay with your grandmother," said Mr. Knottleweed-Eversprightly.

Elly's heart sank. Grandmother Knottle-weed-Eversprightly has strong ideas about the way young fairies should—and shouldn't—behave. And she doesn't like the way Elly behaves one little bit.

"But your grandmother seems to be away," continued Mrs. Knottleweed-Eversprightly. "She's not answering her wand messages."

Elly tried not to smile. Finally, some good news!

"But," said her father, "there is another possibility. Cherrydale Fairy Academy has a vacancy."

Elly looked at her parents in horror. Cherrydale is a fairy boarding school. A very *strict* boarding school. It is so strict that students are only allowed to let their feet touch the ground three times a day. And they have to wear their uniforms on the weekends, too.

Elly started thinking. It was the sort of thinking you do when you have to come up with a solution very quickly. The sort of thinking that makes whirring sounds come out of your ears. Elly wasn't ready to give up just yet. She really wanted to go undercover at a human school. There *had* to be something she could do to get there.

Chapter two

Elly's brain whirred for a while. Then it started grinding. Then finally, it made a *bing*! sound, because Elly had an idea. It seemed like the perfect solution to her, but sometimes it took adult fairies a little while to catch on to good ideas.

You may have had the same trouble with adult humans.

"Mom," said Elly. "I could stay with Jess's family while you're away."

Elly could see from her parents' faces that they were going to be slow to catch on to this good idea. So, she kept explaining. "It's perfect for an undercover operation! And I'll learn so much about humans if I live with a human family," she said. "It will be good research for being a better fairy. I might even be able to put some of the things I discover into the Human Research Database."

But Elly's parents were being stubborn.

"I don't know," said Mrs. Knottleweed-Eversprightly. "I'd feel better if you were staying with fairies. It's not that I don't like humans, it's just that they're different from us."

Elly decided to use another tactic. Cold, hard facts. "Cherrydale is a really strict school, Mom," she said. "And I haven't had much luck at strict schools, remember?"

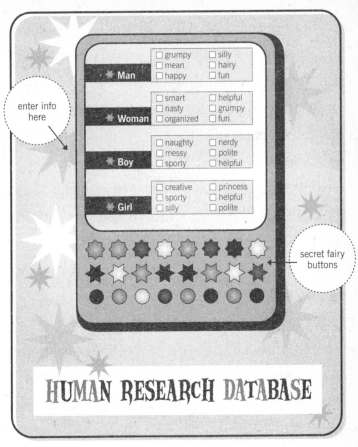

enter info here

secret fairy buttons

HUMAN RESEARCH DATABASE

This was true. It wasn't that Elly *meant* to get into trouble. It just seemed to happen.

"Imagine," said Elly, "if I get thrown out of Cherrydale while you're away. What will happen to me then?"

Mrs. and Mr. Knottleweed-Eversprightly looked at each other.

"Wellll . . ." said Elly's mom.

Elly knew that when her mom said "Wellll . . ." like that, it meant she was starting to come around to Elly's way of thinking.

"Well, that's true," her mom continued. "But I've never even met Jess's parents. We can't leave you with total strangers."

Elly smiled. The hard part of the convincing was done. "Let's go over and meet them then!" she said. "You'll like the Chesters; I know you will."

Half an hour later, the Knottleweed-Eversprightlys were sitting in their neighbors'

living room, drinking tea and eating shortbread cookies that tasted just a tiny bit like mud. Mrs. Chester was a potter and Mr. Chester was a gardener, so dirt just seemed to get into everything. Elly could tell that her parents were a bit nervous about being in a human house. Elly understood. She had felt that way too when she'd first visited Jess.

Human houses are so different from fairy ones, and it is easy to make stupid blunders. For instance, human doors don't allow you to walk straight through them the way fairy ones do. Mr. Knottleweed-Eversprightly almost banged into a closed door before he remembered to open it manually. It was also weird that human furniture stayed in the same place. Fairy furniture has a tendency to wander around. Elly liked human furniture

much more. She was sick of tripping over unexpected things hiding in the dark. To make it worse, fairy furniture always acts like it's your fault. On the whole, Elly felt much happier being in the Chesters's house than she did in her own.

The only thing Elly was really worried about during the visit was Kara. Elly had already caught her making the teapot rise up and start to tip. Elly stopped it just in time. She didn't want anything to happen that might turn the Chesters off the idea of her staying with them.

But if the Chesters noticed any strange goings-on, they didn't say anything.

"Of course Elly can stay with us!" said Mrs. Chester. "We'd love to have her."

"We'll set up the spare bed in Jess's room,"

said Mr. Chester.

Jess and Elly looked at each other in delight. Elly's parents looked relieved. In fact, the only person who didn't look happy about it was Jess's little brother, Micky. "Great," he muttered. "Now, I'm going to have *two* big sisters bossing me around."

After this had been arranged, things happened very fast. The Knottleweed-Eversprightlys hurried home to finish packing, and by early afternoon, they were ready to leave. Elly and the Chester family stood on the sidewalk to wave them good-bye.

"It looks very squished in there," said Mrs. Chester, sympathetically, looking at the Knottleweed-Eversprightlys's station wagon.

From the outside, it looked as if the car was almost completely full. Only Elly knew

that inside the car, it was much more roomy.
There was a bathroom. And a sauna. There was
even a very small movie theater.

"Bye!" called Elly, as the car drove off. She felt a bit sad. It was exciting to be staying with Jess, but she'd miss her family, too. Her own bag was packed and laying by her feet. Once the car had disappeared, Jess picked her bag up.

"Come on," she said. "Let's go and unpack. I've cleared some space for your stuff in my closet."

Elly immediately started feeling better. Elly's mom had told her to pack carefully. Now that she was working undercover, she was only supposed to take the most ordinary of her belongings, and even her wand had to be left behind.

"No one can ever find out you are a fairy," Mrs. Knottleweed-Eversprightly had warned. "Not even Jess."

21

Elly had blushed a little. Her mom didn't know that Jess already knew all about it. "I'll be on my best behavior," she had promised.

Jess's room looked a bit like a cross between a science lab and a factory. She had her chemistry set on her desk and lots of tools on her shelves. The only way you could tell it was a girl's bedroom was by the posters of Jess's favorite bands. Elly thought Jess's room was cool, especially all the half-finished inventions lying around. When they walked in, Elly spotted something fluttering on Jess's desk. At first, she thought a small bird was trapped inside, but when she got closer, she saw that it was just a pen. But not a normal pen. A pen with wings!

"It's my latest experiment," explained Jess. "Once it's working properly, I'm going to train

it to come when I call."

"What a great idea!" said Elly.

Jess sighed. "It would be if I could actually get it to work. All it does at the moment is roll around."

Jess helped Elly unpack. Elly had brought all her favorite clothes—there wasn't a single pink or scratchy thing! Right at the bottom of Elly's bag was a small package. Elly recognized her mom's writing on the card.

This will look after you while we're away, the card said.

Elly unwrapped the package.

"What is it?" Jess asked.

"A watch," said Elly, showing her. "But knowing my mom, it's probably not a normal watch."

She picked the watch up and instantly

the strap locked around her wrist. This was surprising enough, but it was even more astonishing when the watch spoke. It had a mechanical, worried sort of voice.

WORRY WATCH

"Are you eating well?" it asked, anxiously. "You look thin."

Elly groaned. Now she knew what this was—a Worry Watch. She quickly tried to undo it, but the clip held securely.

"Sorry," said the Worry Watch. "You're not authorized to undo me."

"Is that thing actually talking to you?" asked Jess, curiously.

Elly nodded. "It's just like having a worried parent around, all day long."

"That's going to get really annoying," said Jess.

"Yes," agreed Elly. "It is."

chapter three

T he Worry Watch woke the girls up at 6:30 the next morning.

"LOOK OUT!" it yelled.

Elly sat up with a start. "What?" she asked, looking around sleepily. "What happened?"

Everything seemed perfectly normal. She looked at the watch on her wrist. It seemed to be smirking.

"Time to get up," said the watch.

"What's wrong with just a simple 'good

morning'?" grumbled Jess, who was also no.
awake.

"It's your first day at your new school," said the watch, ignoring Jess. "Don't be late."

"You're more of a Bossy Watch than a Worry Watch," complained Elly, but she got up anyway.

Elly had never used a human shower before. At home, she either took a bath or, if she was in a hurry, cleaned herself with a dirt-absorbing towel. She didn't really like using the dirt-absorbing towels because they liked to flick your legs when you weren't watching. The shower, thought Elly, was much better. "It's like having your own rain cloud, but warmer," she said to Jess.

Jess was already dressed by the time Elly got out. She was wearing jeans.

Elly looked at her in surprise. "Don't you have to wear a uniform?" she asked.

Jess shook her head. "We can wear whatever we like," she said.

Elly wasn't sure if she believed Jess, but she put on her favorite clothes anyway. With her wings safely tucked away beneath her

clothes, she looked exactly like a human kid. No one would ever guess her secret.

"Is this OK?" she asked Jess.

"Perfect!" Jess said. "Do you need to borrow a backpack?"

"No, thanks," she said. "I've got one." She showed Jess her small red backpack.

Jess looked at it doubtfully. "It's a bit small," she said.

But Elly shook her head. "Anything I put in it gets shrunk," she explained. "So, it actually fits a lot more than you'd think."

To demonstrate, Elly reached into the bag and pulled out her skateboard.

Jess was impressed. "Cool," she said. "How does it work?"

"It sucks the moisture out of things," Elly said. "Think of a dried apricot. Then it puts the

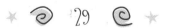

moisture back in when you take stuff out."

After breakfast, the girls set off for school on their bikes. Elly had brought her bike from home. It was just like a human bike, except it had a special Fairy Drive setting. In Fairy Drive, it turned into a Glider Bike and began moving very quickly. As they got closer to the school, Elly started seeing more and more kids. Some were on bikes and some were walking. There were even some kids riding skateboards. They all looked so different from the students at a fairy school.

"What are the kids in our class like?" Elly asked Jess. Suddenly, Elly missed her best friend, Saphie, who was also a fairy. She couldn't wait to tell her all about human school.

Jess made a face. "They are really different

from the kids at my old school," said Jess. Jess had only been going to South Street School for a little while. "All the girls are into fairies. They have this Fairy Club and they act like fairies are the best thing in the world." Suddenly, Jess realized what she'd said. "Sorry," she said. "Sometimes I forget that you're a fairy."

"That's OK," said Elly. "I forget, too."

There were lots of kids already at South Street School, running around, playing games, laughing and talking. It was very noisy—much noisier than a fairy school, and much busier, too. Just walking across the playground was like crossing an obstacle course. Balls were flying in all directions.

"WATCH OUT!" shrieked the Worry Watch, whizzing its hands around frantically.

Elly looked up just in time to see a soccer ball heading right for her head. Without thinking, Elly tried to fly away, forgetting her wings were safely tucked underneath her clothes. She fell flat on her face and the ball sailed over her head.

Elly noticed the playground had gone quiet. Everyone was staring at her. Jess helped her to her feet. She was pale.

"We're going to have to do something

about that watch," she said. "It's going to draw too much attention to you."

Elly examined the watchband. She could just fit one finger under it.

"Maybe we can cut it off," she suggested.

"No way!" shrilled the watch, and tightened itself even more firmly around Elly's wrist. "There's no way you—" it began to say, but Elly clamped her hand over its face. The watch stopped talking mid-sentence.

"That's interesting," said Jess. She pulled the ribbon off the end of her braid. "Tie this around the watch. Maybe if it can't see anything, it stops worrying. Like an ostrich with its head in the sand."

Elly tied the ribbon around the watch. Then she pretended to trip over a rock. Sure enough, the watch stayed silent.

"Phew!" said Elly, gratefully. Jess was good at solving stuff like this.

"Come on," said Jess. "I'll show you around."

Jess took Elly to her locker, which was right next to hers. Out of habit, Elly bent over and put her eye up against the keyhole. She waited patiently.

"What *are* you doing?" laughed Jess.

"I'm doing an eyeball scan to open my locker," said Elly.

"We don't do it that way here," said Jess. "We use these." She unhooked a small silver key hanging from the handle of the locker.

Elly felt silly. She'd thought it would be easy to act like a human, mainly because she'd never felt like a proper fairy. But being a human wasn't so easy after all. She looked around to see if anyone had seen her. Someone had. A girl was standing behind her, staring. The girl had curly brown hair and big brown eyes. Elly wondered if she would be in her class. She smiled at the girl, but the girl just kept staring.

"Found yourself a friend who's just as weird as you?" she called out to Jess. Pinned to her sweater was a pink, sparkly badge with the letters FC.

"She's not weird, she's interesting," retorted Jess. "Which is more than I can say about you, Clarabelle."

The girl looked annoyed. "You'll never get into Fairy Club if you keep saying stuff like that," she said, tossing her head.

Jess sighed. "That would be really terrible, Clarabelle," she said, "if I actually *wanted* to be in Fairy Club." Jess closed her locker. "But I don't."

Elly watched the girl as she walked away, her perfect ponytail swinging. She was shocked. *What if all humans are like this girl?*

"That's Clarabelle Honkeybottom," Jess said.

Elly started to laugh. "*Honkeybottom?*" she said.

Jess grinned. "I know. It's terrible, isn't it? She thinks everyone wants to be in Fairy

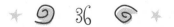

Club, even though I keep telling her I couldn't think of anything worse than dressing up in a tutu and running around waving a wand in the air."

Elly nodded, but she kept quiet. She would never admit it to Jess, but she couldn't help feeling just a bit curious about what went on in Fairy Club.

Chapter Four

Elly decided she'd better start watching Jess very carefully so she didn't make any more mistakes. If her true identity were discovered, she would be in trouble with the Fairydom authorities. Staying undercover was part of the deal with her placement.

Jess took her to their classroom. Elly watched how Jess pulled the chair away from the desk and sat down. It was a good thing she was paying attention. She would've looked pretty silly standing there, waiting

for the chair to slide back automatically the way they do in fairy schools.

Clarabelle was already there, sitting with some other girls. All of them seemed to be wearing something pink. One had pink-and-white stockings on, and another was wearing a pink headband. Another girl had light pink jeans on with dark pink flowers all over them. And all of them were wearing the same small pink badge that Elly had noticed on Clarabelle.

The door opened and another girl walked in. She had very green eyes and long, wavy red hair with small flowers braided into it. She was wearing pink, too, but unlike the others— who were wearing one or two pink things— this girl was dressed *entirely* in pink. She had a long pink skirt on with a shorter pink skirt over the top. Her top was pink and her jacket had pink polka dots. She was even wearing a string of pink glass beads around her neck and tiny pink flower earrings. She was so pink that, at first, Elly didn't even notice that she, too, was wearing the small pink badge.

The moment the other girls saw her, a chorus started up.

"Caitlin!" they called. "Sit next to me!" Caitlin waved and smiled at them all, and then sat next to Clarabelle.

"That's Caitlin," whispered Jess. "She's the most popular girl in the class. Maybe even in the whole school. Even the teachers love her."

Elly nodded. There were girls like that at fairy schools, too—the ones that everyone wanted as their best friend.

The door opened again and everyone went quiet. *This must be the teacher*, Elly thought. Out of habit, she started climbing onto her desk, which is how fairies greet their teachers in the morning. Once the teacher has said hello, they all glide into the air and fly gracefully back into their seats. Well, most of them fly gracefully. Somehow, Elly often ended up upside down in her chair. Jess grabbed her arm and pulled her down. Elly went red. She'd made yet another mistake.

"Good morning, class," said the teacher.

"Good morning, Ms. Buttercup," chorused the students.

Elly liked Ms. Buttercup right away. She had smiling eyes and walked in a way that was almost like dancing.

"We have a new student today," said Ms. Buttercup. "Come up here, Elly, and tell everyone a little bit about yourself."

Elly looked at Jess nervously as she walked to the front of the room. What should she say? She had already slipped up so many times today that she couldn't afford to make things worse. But the harder she tried, the more she couldn't think of anything to say. She felt like everyone was staring at her—

as though they knew that she was different, and couldn't figure out how.

"What sport do you play?" asked Ms. Buttercup, kindly.

"Um . . ." said Elly, trying to think. She had learned about human sports in Human Studies class at fairy school. Elly remembered thinking that they sounded much more fun than fairy sports. But right now, her mind had gone blank and she could only think of one human sport. She couldn't remember

what sort of sport it was, but she had to say something.

"Sumo wrestling," she blurted out.

Everyone laughed and Ms. Buttercup looked very surprised. "How unusual!" she said.

Elly looked at Jess, who was shaking her head violently and pointing at something in the corner. "And playing baskets," said Elly.

"Baskets?" said Ms. Buttercup, in surprise.

Elly glanced at Jess again, who was now pointing to something else. A ball.

"Basketball!" she said, triumphantly. "I play basketball."

Jess nodded and slumped back into her chair, looking exhausted.

Ms. Buttercup was delighted. "That's great, Elly!" she said. "We have a school basketball team. Our principal, Mrs. Hayman, is the

coach. Maybe you can join."

Elly nodded politely, but she didn't think this would really happen. She had never been any good at fairy sports, so why would she be any better at human ones?

"OK," said Ms. Buttercup, sending Elly back to her seat. "Now it's time for your spelling test."

Elly was surprised. She didn't think humans did spells. She wondered what kind of wands they used.

"Cartwheel," said Ms. Buttercup, and everyone started writing in their notebooks.

"Immediately," said Ms. Buttercup a moment later.

Elly looked at Jess in confusion. What was going on? Was she supposed to do what Ms. Buttercup said? And if so, it was the

weirdest spell she'd ever heard of.

"Just write the words down," whispered Jess.

Elly couldn't believe it. Was this all you had to do in a human spelling test? It seemed way too easy. Perhaps there was some kind of trick.

But there was no trick. When the test was over Ms. Buttercup got them to grade each other's tests. Jess, who was a pretty good speller, got eight out of ten. But Elly got nine out of ten! She couldn't believe it.

"Wow," said Jess. "That's really good for your first-ever spelling test."

The bell rang.

"OK, class," said Ms. Buttercup. "Mrs. Hayman is taking you for a basketball lesson in the gym today. Make sure you get there in time."

"We'd better hurry," said Jess. "The gym is

way over on the other side of the school."

Elly pulled her skateboard out of her bag. "Let's go the easy way," she said.

"Good idea," smiled Jess.

ELLY'S SKATEBOARD

pointy at front to help lower wind resistance

excellent comet design

fin on the back to increase glide

extra-sticky foot grips to help Elly stay on

super-smooth rainbow wheels

She jumped onto the skateboard behind Elly. It had always been a very fast board, but Elly had just put new wheels on it and now it went so fast that blue sparks shot out behind it as the girls zoomed down the corridor.

"Human school is so much better than fairy school," called Elly over her shoulder as they sped along. "And the teachers are way nicer."

Jess was hanging on very tightly to Elly. She knew they weren't actually flying, but a couple of times it really felt as if the wheels were lifting off the ground.

"You've only met one teacher so far," Jess pointed out. "Not all of them are as nice as Ms. Buttercup. Wait until you meet the cooking teacher, Mrs. Snidely—"

Elly took the next corner just a little too

sharply and the two girls crashed straight into someone coming the other way. Elly and Jess fell on the ground. But the person they crashed into remained upright, as if made of concrete.

"What were you saying about Mrs. Snidely?" asked a voice. It sounded exactly how a concrete person might speak. "I'd be very interested to know."

Jess looked flustered. "Hello, Mrs. Snidely," she said. "I was just telling Elly about how much I love your cooking classes."

Mrs. Snidely looked at Elly the way you might look at something smelly you found stuck to your shoe. "Maybe you can also tell Elly that riding skateboards inside is strictly forbidden," said Mrs. Snidely. "If I catch you again, it'll mean instant detention. For a week!"

"Yes, Mrs. Snidely," muttered Jess.

Jess and Elly watched as Mrs. Snidely walked away.

Elly couldn't help smiling. "Human school might be really different from fairy school in lots of ways," said Elly. "But I guess in other ways, they are exactly the same."

Chapter Five

Elly wasn't feeling very confident about the game. She had never played basketball before and she was hopeless at fairy sports. Formation Flying was the worst. It was a compulsory fairy subject, where you learned how to fly through the air as a group, somersaulting and doing loops in unison. It made Elly dizzy.

Then there was Star Grazer—a popular lunchtime game. Hundreds of tiny golden

stars were released into the air. As they whizzed around, leaving sparkling trails behind them, two teams of fairies chased them with nets. You had to scoop up as many as you could before they dissolved. Elly had hated Star Grazer ever since she ended up with her net stuck on her head. She also detested Wings Aloft and Wand Winder. She always seemed to fly in the wrong direction and crash into someone—usually someone on her own team!

So, as she walked out onto the basketball court, Elly was pretty sure she was about to make an idiot of herself—again.

Elly was surprised when she saw Mrs. Hayman. She didn't look anything like the Head Fairies she knew. She was wearing a tracksuit, for one thing. Elly couldn't imagine

a Head Fairy ever wearing a tracksuit. Ms. Buttercup was there, too.

She smiled at Elly. "I've come to watch," she explained. "I was just telling Mrs. Hayman that basketball is your favorite game."

"Oh yes, I love it," lied Elly. She felt bad lying, but maybe it wouldn't be a lie after all— she hadn't actually played yet. Elly sighed. She wasn't holding out much hope.

Mrs. Hayman divided the class into two teams. Elly and Jess were on the blue team. Caitlin and Clarabelle were on the red.

"What am I supposed to do?" Elly whispered to Jess.

"Just follow me," Jess whispered back. "Then try to get the ball through the hoop."

Clarabelle ran past them, bouncing the ball.

"And watch out for Clarabelle," added Jess, frowning. "She cheats."

Elly nodded. She just hoped that humans didn't cheat in the same way that fairies did. Fairies had a habit of turning their opponents into things—like hot dogs or goldfish—when they thought they might lose. It was very unpleasant.

Mrs. Hayman blew her whistle and the game began. Someone threw the ball to Jess and Jess threw it to Elly. For a moment, Elly stood still, looking at the ball. She'd forgotten what to do.

"Run, Elly!" yelled Jess.

And so Elly ran, bouncing the ball the way Clarabelle had. She ran toward the hoop. She was almost there when she realized Clarabelle was approaching fast.

"Just throw the ball to me, weirdo," called Clarabelle. "It'll save me the effort of taking it from you."

Elly looked around. There were no other blue team players close by, and the hoop suddenly looked very far away. What were the chances of her reaching it from here? She'd never made a basket before and Clarabelle was right behind her. Maybe she should just let her have the ball? After all, she would probably just snatch it in a moment anyway.

Elly made up her mind. "Hey, Clarabelle," she said, suddenly. "Catch!"

But instead of throwing the ball to Clarabelle, Elly aimed for the hoop. She sprung up as high off the ground as she could and kept her arm steady as the ball left her

hands. The ball started veering off to the left, far away from the hoop.

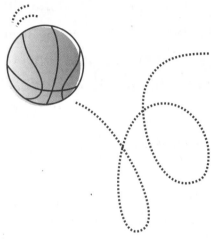

Clarabelle watched.

"There's no way that one's going in," she sniggered.

But the ball suddenly screeched to a stop in midair. Instead of going to the left, it began curving to the right. Then, while the whole class watched in astonishment, the basketball

plopped down through the middle of the hoop.

"NO WAY!" said Clarabelle, in disbelief.

The blue team players jumped up and down in excitement. Everyone, that is, except Jess and Elly. They looked at each other.

"Are you using magic?" Jess whispered to Elly, suspiciously.

Elly shook her head. "I'm not, I swear," she said.

"Well, how can you explain what just happened?" asked Jess.

But Elly couldn't explain it. Something strange was going on, but she wasn't quite sure what.

For the rest of the game, Elly tried to avoid the ball. But somehow, it always ended up in her hands. And when she tried to throw it to

someone else—even someone on the other team—it always ended up going through the hoop. Finally, she tried throwing the ball while facing the wrong way. Standing on one foot. With her eyes closed.

She had a feeling she knew what was going on. If she got this basket, she knew she would be right. There was a moment of silence, and then the cheers of the blue team told her that she had got the ball through the hoop.

Finally, Mrs. Hayman blew her whistle. "Game over," she said. "Congratulations, blue team! Good work, Elly. You've definitely earned a place on the school basketball team. You are very talented."

"Oh, not really," said Elly, modestly. She could see that Clarabelle was looking at her suspiciously. "I was just lucky."

Jess looked at her friend admiringly as they headed toward the changing room.

"You're a natural at basketball," she said.

Elly looked around. "I don't think I am a natural," she said quietly, "but I do think that I'm not the only fairy at South Street School."

Chapter Six

At lunchtime, Elly and Jess talked about what had happened. They had to talk softly because Caitlin, Clarabelle, and the rest of the Fairy Club girls were sitting nearby.

"That wasn't a normal ball," said Elly. "There was definitely a fairy gadget involved somehow."

Jess was wide-eyed. "So, you think someone else in our class is an undercover fairy?"

Elly nodded. "I'm sure of it," she said. "And

we're going to find out who it is."

Jess was excited. "We'll be like detectives!" she said. "Let's look for clues."

Elly shook her head. She was hungry. "Let's have lunch first. You should never look for clues on an empty stomach."

She opened her backpack and pulled out a large, glittery blue box.

"What's that?" asked Jess, curiously. It looked a bit like a lunch box with a big dial on top.

"It's a Wunch Box," explained Elly. "Wunch stands for Whatever U Need Culinary Holder," she said, and showed Jess how the box worked.

On the dial were numerous lunchtime options—from sandwiches to pizza slices. All you have to do is turn the dial to what you

WUNCH BOX

Whatever you want!

Pizza slice appears magically!

Wunch Box dial options

63

want for lunch, and when you open the box, there it is, waiting for you.

"You put the ingredient powder in here," said Elly, opening up a flap on the side. "And you have to charge it up once a week."

"That's a cool invention," said Jess. She liked her mom's pottery, but she couldn't help wishing that she were an inventor, like Elly's mom.

"It's good if it's working properly," said Elly. She'd had trouble with her Wunch Box before, and today it was looking particularly dented and scratched.

Elly felt like tomato soup. But when she tried turning the dial, she found it wouldn't budge from cupcakes.

"That's not so bad," said Jess, looking at the options on the dial. "It could've been

stuck on olive and anchovy pancakes."

Elly sighed. Cupcakes were fine if you were in the mood for them. But she felt like tomato soup. Unfortunately, it looked like it was cupcakes or nothing. There was nothing she could do but click the "Make Lunch!" button, and wait.

A few moments later, steam began to rise from the Wunch Box and the smell of baking filled the air. The Fairy Club girls looked up when the cupcake smell wafted over. Caitlin looked at Elly and Jess curiously. Elly waved her hands around, hoping to make the smell go away.

Caitlin smiled and waved back. "Your lunch smells great!" she called.

"Thanks!" Elly called back.

"You know," Elly said to Jess, "I don't think

Caitlin's all that bad."

Jess shrugged. "She's not as bad as most of the Fairy Club girls, I guess."

"What exactly *is* Fairy Club?" asked Elly.

"I guess they just sit around talking about fairies," Jess said. Then she looked quickly at Elly. "Not cool fairies like you, of course. Silly fairies."

Elly nodded. She knew all about silly fairy stuff.

"Then on the weekend, they go to each other's houses and dress up and pretend they're fairies," continued Jess, rolling her eyes. "It's so dumb."

Jess seemed to know a lot about Fairy Club. "Have you ever been?" Elly asked her.

Jess looked embarrassed. "Well, no," she said. "But I'm glad. I wouldn't want to go

anyway. I'd rather spend my spare time inventing a flying machine."

Elly opened the Wunch Box and a row of perfect cupcakes was sitting inside, covered in chocolate icing and colored sprinkles. She offered one to Jess.

"Wow!" said Jess, taking one. "They look great."

"Let me try mine first," warned Elly, sniffing her cake. "Sometimes the Wunch Box food isn't quite right. Once, I had a banana that tasted like salami. It was so disgusting." Elly took a cautious bite and smiled. This time, at least, the cupcake was perfect.

Jess took a big bite of hers. "These are great!" she said. She picked up the Wunch Box and examined it closely. "Maybe I could turn my lunch box into one of these. What is

the ingredient powder made of?"

"Kitchen dust," said Elly.

Jess spat out a mouthful of cake. "Dust?" she repeated in disgust. "That's so gross!"

"Not really," said Elly. "Mom worked out that dust is just tiny flakes of stuff from around the house. She fills the Wunch Box up with dust she has collected from the kitchen and the Wunch Box just sorts through the pieces." She took another bite. "Plus, it's not human dust. It's fairy dust, which is much cleaner."

Jess looked at the remains of the cupcake in her hand. It didn't look nearly so delicious anymore. "I think I'll just stick with my sandwich," she said. She didn't fancy eating dust food no matter whose dust had been used. Dust food was the sort of thing you only gave to people you didn't like.

This gave Jess an idea. She nudged Elly. "I dare you to go and offer them to Fairy Club," she said, smiling mischievously.

Elly got up. "Good idea!" she said. "We've got way too many here." And she walked over to the Fairy Club girls before Jess could stop her.

Jess stopped smiling and started feeling bad. She hoped the dustcakes weren't poisonous. She watched as the Fairy Club girls each chose a cake. She could tell from their faces that Elly hadn't told them what the key ingredient was. She could also see that they thought the cakes were delicious. Especially Caitlin. Once she'd finished her first cake, she took another one. Jess saw her say something to Elly. Then she handed her a

piece of paper. *What on earth could it be?*

Elly rushed back a moment later, looking very excited. "Caitlin's invited us to a Fairy Club meeting this weekend!" she said.

Jess shook her head. "No way," she said, firmly. "I refuse to go to some stupid fairy party."

Elly hopped around on one foot. "But Jess, I really, *really* want to go. She's even given us an invitation," she said, holding it out. It was pink and covered in little gold wands and stars. Looking at the invitation made Jess want to go even less. But it was hard to say no when your friend was so excited.

"We'd have to dress up, you know," Jess warned Elly.

Elly nodded enthusiastically. "I've always wanted to go to a costume party!" she said.

You are invited
to a
Fairy Club meeting
on Saturday
at Caitlin's house

Jess sighed. "You don't get it," she said. "We'd have to dress up as *fairies*."

But even this didn't seem to worry Elly.

"I don't understand why you're so excited to go to a fairy party," Jess said. "I thought you hated all that stuff."

Elly nodded. "I do," she said. "But when you're a detective, you sometimes have to do things you don't want to do."

Jess looked at Elly suspiciously. She wondered if Elly was trying to trick her. "Have you found a clue?" she asked.

Elly leaned in and whispered in her ear. "Have you noticed that for someone with very pale skin, Caitlin hardly has any freckles?"

Jess stared at her.

"And that her hair is really, really shiny?" Elly added.

Jess felt a shiver of excitement. She looked over at Caitlin and noticed for the first time that she was much shorter than any of the other Fairy Club girls.

"You think she's a . . . ?" she whispered.

Elly shrugged. "That's what we're going to find out on Saturday," she said.

Chapter Seven

The first class after lunch was cooking with Mrs. Snidely. Elly decided to try very hard in this class to get on Mrs. Snidely's good side. Since the skateboard incident in the hallway, she had a feeling that the cooking teacher didn't really like her very much.

"Don't worry," Jess said, as they walked to class. "Cooking is pretty fun, really, even if it is with Mrs. Snidely. And it's easy."

But Elly wasn't so sure. "It's the boy fairies

that do most of the cooking in Fairydom," she explained. Some girl fairies were good at cooking, but Elly wasn't one of them. It was a bit too much like doing spells for her liking—all that "pinch of this, splash of that" stuff. Elly tended to get the pinches muddled up with the splashes. In fact, the only food that Elly could cook was party food.

Mrs. Snidely was waiting for them when they arrived, wearing a neat white apron that looked brand new. Written on the board behind her was a recipe.

"Today," announced Mrs. Snidely, "we are going to make sausage rolls. Work in pairs and follow the recipe on the board."

Elly was relieved. Party food! Maybe this wouldn't be so hard after all. "We won't need to follow the recipe," Elly said confidently to

Jess. "I've made sausage rolls loads of times."

"Are you sure?" said Jess. "Human sausage rolls might be different."

Elly laughed. "How different could they be?" she asked.

Elly measured out the ingredients while Jess did the mixing. Caitlin and Clarabelle were working on the next counter down, and Elly could tell that Clarabelle was working extra hard to try and beat them. But they didn't know the recipe and had to keep looking at the board. It wasn't long before Elly and Jess were miles ahead.

"I can't believe you had so much trouble at fairy school," said Jess. "You're practically the best student here already."

Elly felt embarrassed. She wasn't used to being told she was good at things, especially school things. Even Mrs. Snidely looked impressed when she came over to inspect the trays. She put the tray in the oven and turned on the timer.

"Let me know when they're done," she said,

looking hungrily at Jess and Elly's sausage rolls as she shut the door. "I'll come over and try one."

Elly smiled. Jess had been right. Cooking *was* fun. It was much more fun than fairy cooking. Fairy kitchens have lots of appliances, but sometimes the appliances make things harder rather than easier. Like the fairy mixing bowl. It was designed to really enjoy mixing things, but the problem is it enjoys mixing so much that it often doesn't want you to take the mixture out! It just keeps stirring and stirring and if you get too close, it splatters you with batter. The human mixing bowls seemed much better behaved.

When the oven timer rang, everyone gathered around. Jess lifted out the tray.

"Wow," said Caitlin. "They look so great!"

It was true. The sausage rolls were golden brown on top and smelled great.

"I'd better try the first one," said Mrs. Snidely, pushing to the front of the crowd. "Just in case anything is wrong with them."

But as she reached toward the biggest, juiciest sausage roll, something very unusual happened. The roll began to roll! It moved slowly at first, but the closer Mrs. Snidely's hand got, the faster it rolled. Mrs. Snidely pulled her hand away in fright. The roll stopped rolling.

Mrs. Snidely shook her head. "I must have imagined it," she muttered to herself. She cautiously reached her hand out again. But the moment she got close, the sausage roll began to roll again, this time at *double* the speed.

Jess looked at Elly in alarm. "Did you put a spell on them?" Jess whispered.

"They're sausage *rolls*," Elly whispered back. "That's what they're *supposed* to do, isn't it?"

Jess rolled her eyes. She should've known better than to follow a fairy's cooking instructions. "Generally, humans prefer food that stays still," she said.

Jess looked around at her classmates. Did they know what was going on? A few people were laughing, but most of the faces in the kitchen wore shocked expressions. And the most shocked expression of all was on the face of their teacher.

Mrs. Snidely turned and glared at Elly and Jess. "Would either of you care to tell me what's going on?" she said sharply. "I suspect

funny business and I don't like it. Not one bit."

But before the girls could say anything, the door opened and Ms. Buttercup's smiling face popped around the corner.

"It smells great in here," she said. "What's cooking?"

"That," said Mrs. Snidely, "is precisely what I'm trying to find out."

She had taken several steps away from the tray and was looking at it as if she was afraid the sausage rolls might leap off the tray and attack her. Ms. Buttercup walked cautiously over to the counter. She reached out her hand and, sure enough, the rolls began to roll wildly. Ms. Buttercup frowned for a moment. Then, she smiled.

"Oh, I get it," she said. "The tray is on a

slope. See?"

Everyone looked. It was true. One edge of the tray was resting on a lump of pastry.

"That's obviously causing the sausage rolls to roll around like that."

Mrs. Snidely shook her head. "That's utterly illogical," she said sternly.

But Ms. Buttercup didn't seem to hear her. She lifted the tray and removed the lump of pastry.

"There," she said, and reached out toward the sausage rolls again. Everyone held their breath, but the sausage rolls didn't budge. Ms. Buttercup picked one up and took a bite.

"Delicious!" she announced, smiling at Elly and Jess.

Mrs. Snidely looked puzzled. "That doesn't make sense. . . . "

"Have one, Mrs. Snidely," urged Ms. Buttercup.

Mrs. Snidely looked like she really didn't want to go anywhere near the oddly behaving sausage rolls. But everyone was watching her. Mrs. Snidely took a deep breath and gingerly stretched out her hand. The rolls stayed put. She picked one up and, once she was convinced that it wasn't going anywhere, took a cautious nibble.

"Not bad," she said eventually. "But they need a pinch more salt."

Chapter Eight

After that, Jess kept a watchful eye on Elly, and somehow they managed to get through the rest of the day without any more disasters. It kept Jess very busy though, and she didn't have any time to think about Caitlin's party. But as they biked home that afternoon, Jess started worrying about it again.

"Maybe you could go without me," she suggested.

But Elly shook her head. "A good detective

needs a partner," she said.

Jess sighed. She had a feeling Elly would say that. And she was quite looking forward to being a detective. That, at least, sounded like fun.

But there was one other problem. "I don't have anything to wear," she said. It was true. Jess's clothes could not have been less like fairy clothes if she'd tried.

But Elly had already thought of that. "It's OK," she said. "We're going to stop at my place. I've got loads of things that will be perfect."

"Really?" said Jess. She had always wanted to see inside Elly's house.

But when they pulled up outside number 27 Raspberry Drive, Jess wasn't so sure anymore. The house looked very dark. Jess

stood behind Elly as she unlocked the front door and they both peered inside.

Jess was amazed at what she saw. "Everything's tiny!" she exclaimed.

It was true. Just inside the door was a normal-sized room, but beyond that, the house looked like it was made for dolls.

"Oh, I forgot to tell you," said Elly. "We always shrink the house when we go away."

Jess was puzzled. "But it looks the same size from the outside," she said.

Elly smiled. "Pretty convincing, isn't it?" she said. "But I wouldn't lean on it. It's not really there at all."

Something occurred to Jess. "Does this mean we can't get the fairy outfits?" she asked.

Elly shook her head. "No, it just means

that we'll have to shrink ourselves with the Anatomical Re-sizer."

Jess looked around the normal-sized entrance hall. There was a lamp and a painting but nothing that looked like it might be an Anatomical Re-sizer, whatever *that* was.

"Where is it?" she asked.

Elly pulled Jess into the entrance hall and closed the front door. "We're standing in it," she said, lifting the painting off the wall.

Hidden behind it was a panel of glowing buttons and dials. Elly pressed one and immediately the lamp lit up with an eerie red glow that slowly turned purple, then orange.

Elly looked at her friend. "Are you scared?" she asked.

"No, but what will shrinking feel like?"

ANATOMICAL RE-SIZER

lamp has eerie red glow

glowing lights and panels

asked Jess. Adventures were cool, but she wasn't so keen on getting hurt.

"It just tingles a bit," said Elly. "And your stomach drops like when you're on a swing."

Jess nodded. That sounded OK. "Let's shrink!" she said.

Elly pushed one of the buttons. The lamp flashed purple and suddenly it felt as if the walls were rocketing up into the air. At the same time, the floorboards seemed to be getting closer and closer. The wind whistled furiously in their ears. And then, everything stopped as suddenly as it had started.

It was very still. Jess looked around. It didn't feel like anything had happened at all. She felt exactly the same. Elly looked the same, too. But then Jess looked down the hall to where she had seen all the tiny furniture. It wasn't tiny anymore. Everything looked normal size.

"Come on," said Elly. "We should hurry."

She led the way down the hall. The house was very dark and just a little bit spooky. Jess kept thinking she could see things hiding in the corners, but when she got closer, it would turn out to be a bookcase or a chair. But then when she turned away, she couldn't help feeling that the things were moving. Jess felt better once her eyes got used to the dark.

They were standing near a staircase that curled up into the darkness. "My room is up there," said Elly, as she started climbing. Jess followed behind her.

Halfway up the stairs, Elly stopped. "Did you hear that?" she whispered.

Jess stood still and listened. Her heart was

beating very fast all of a sudden. She heard a noise, too.

"Stay there," said Elly.

Elly tiptoed toward her bedroom door, which was slightly ajar. Jess didn't really want to be on her own, but she didn't want to go into the bedroom either. In fact, she just wanted to leave. The noise started again. It sounded like something bumping and crashing into the walls. *What could it possibly be?* It might be just a beetle or a fly. Jess wasn't scared of bugs when they were so much smaller than she was. But now that she had been shrunk, she wasn't sure she would like to run into one the same size as her.

Elly disappeared into the bedroom. Jess gripped the banister very tightly. She wished she hadn't agreed to come. From inside the

room came a very loud buzzing sound and a number of crashes and thumps. Jess froze. Maybe it was a bee or a wasp! Should she run in and help Elly or should she run away? But then she heard Elly laughing.

"Oh, it's you!" Elly exclaimed. Her head

popped back around the door. "Don't worry, Jess," she said. "It's just my Hover Lamp."

Jess walked cautiously into the room. She

ducked as something whirred past her ear. "What's a Hover Lamp?" she asked.

"Hang on," said Elly. "I'll turn it on."

She gave a piercing whistle and immediately the room was flooded with a soft, golden light. The lamp flew above Jess's head and circled around three times. It finally landed on her shoulder. It nuzzled into Jess's neck and made a sort of mechanical purring noise in her ear. Jess laughed. She wasn't nervous anymore.

"It's a pretty cute lamp!" she said.

Elly smiled. "I think it likes you," she said.

Elly swung open her closet doors. Inside, it was bursting with clothes—shiny pink skirts, sequin-covered tops, and frilly white sleeves fought each other for space.

"How come you've got so many clothes?" asked Jess, surprised.

"Most of them are school uniforms," explained Elly. "And you know how many schools I've been to."

She threw some outfits on the bed. First was a lilac dress with a big flouncy skirt and tiny rosebuds sewn along the hem. Then there was a pale, shimmery blue dress with an enormous white satin bow on the back.

"How about this one?" said Elly, holding up a dress. It was a long pink tutu, embroidered with tiny silver stars. Each star had a glittering diamond in the middle. "It's even got a matching tiara!" said Elly, holding up a crown of stars.

Jess looked at the outfit in horror. "There's no way I'm wearing that!" she said.

94

Elly sighed. "But this is the perfect disguise," she explained. "No one will guess that you're actually a fairy detective if you're dressed like this."

"No," agreed Jess. "They wouldn't think I was a detective because they'd be too busy thinking I was completely insane."

But Elly wasn't listening. She had found something else in the closet.

"Are they wings?" asked Jess, when Elly handed them to her.

"Wing protectors," said Elly. "School fairies wear them over their real wings when it rains. If we pin them to your back, they'll look just like real wings."

Jess sighed. "Do you really want to do this?" she asked.

She could think of so many better things

to do on Saturday than dress up in one of these uncomfortable-looking dresses. But Elly had made up her mind.

"I can't think of a better place to catch a fairy," she said firmly, "than at a fairy party."

Chapter Nine

U sually, when you are looking forward to something on the weekend—like a party—the days in between can seem very long. But for Elly, the rest of the week flew by. She was very busy with her new classes and basketball practice. And as she got used to being at a human school, she stopped making so many embarrassing mistakes.

Then before she knew it, it was Saturday morning and the Worry Watch was waking

her up in its typical, rude way.

"WATCH OUT!" it yelled. "THE PARTY'S TODAY!"

Jess groaned and put her pillow over her head. The Hover Lamp flew over and sat on her chest. It had refused to stay behind at the house and the girls had ended up resizing it and sneaking it into the Chesters's house with them.

"Is that watch ever going to run out of batteries?" Jess asked.

"Unfortunately not," said Elly. "It runs on body heat, so as long as I'm wearing it, it'll keep going. And as you know," she added, giving the band a tug, "I've already tried to undo it."

"Don't bother," said the Worry Watch, holding on grimly.

Elly enjoyed getting ready for the party. She had decided to wear the lilac dress with the flouncy skirt. There was a matching garland of rosebuds that she wove into her hair. Whenever she'd worn this outfit before, she'd found it scratchy and uncomfortable. Today, though, things were different. Because the dress was now a disguise rather than a uniform, it suddenly seemed much less itchy.

She poked her wings through the wing-holes and fluttered them. It felt good to stretch them after they'd been trapped beneath her clothes all week. As a final touch, she unwound the ribbon that had been hiding the Worry Watch during school hours.

"No panicking, OK?" she told it sternly.

The watch whizzed its arms around, but didn't make any promises.

Jess didn't seem to be enjoying herself quite so much. "Maybe I could be a plain clothes fairy detective," she suggested, looking down at the fairy dress she was wearing. "I'm just going to fall over all the time in this thing."

But Elly insisted that it was better if she was dressed as a fairy. Then she made her stand still while she turned her hair into a mass of tiny little curls.

"This is how fairies wear their hair at parties," Elly explained. Then she pinned on the wing protectors and stepped back to look at Jess. Elly couldn't help laughing. "You look exactly like a fairy!" she said. "Just a very grumpy one."

"I feel stupid," said Jess.

Elly shrugged. "Sometimes you have to do stuff like this when you're a detective," she said.

The Hover Lamp tried to follow them as they left. Elly put it firmly back on the bedside table. "Sorry," she said, "but I think a flying, flashing lamp might just blow our cover."

The lamp blinked its lights and made a whiney noise. But Elly insisted. "Stay!" said Elly, and closed the door carefully behind them.

Caitlin lived a couple of streets away, so the girls rode there on Elly's skateboard. Jess held on tight to Elly's backpack.

"I hope no one sees us," said Jess, nervously.

"Don't worry," said Elly. "We'll be at the party soon and everyone will look just like we do."

But the girls were in for a surprise. When they arrived at Caitlin's house, the first person they saw was Clarabelle. She was wearing jeans. She looked at Elly and Jess in surprise, but before she could say anything, Caitlin appeared. She was wearing jeans, too, and, even more surprisingly, her T-shirt looked like it had an oil stain on it.

Elly and Jess looked around. They were the only guests dressed as fairies.

"Hi, guys," said Caitlin. "Cool outfits!"

Elly frowned. "Isn't this a fairy party?" she said. "I thought we had to dress up."

Caitlin smiled. "No," she said. "We just wear normal stuff. Those fairy outfits are too uncomfortable. And besides, they'd get dirty when we work on our inventions."

"Inventions?" Jess repeated.

Caitlin nodded. "That's the whole point of Fairy Club," she explained. "At the moment, we're working on how to make things fly."

Jess and Elly looked at each other. This was not how they had imagined Fairy Club at all.

Caitlin saw their surprised expressions. "What did you think Fairy Club was about? Running around with wings, waving wands?" she said, laughing.

Elly and Jess didn't say anything because that was *exactly* what they had thought.

"We're about to start working," said Caitlin. "Get something to eat from the table if you're hungry." She pointed to a card table piled high with food. "It's all *fairy*-type food," she said, apologetically. "My mom thinks that's what we should be eating at Fairy Club. She thinks we're still little kids."

Elly and Jess went over to the table. "What is all this stuff?" Elly asked Jess.

She had never seen so much pink food in her life.

Caitlin pointed to the different plates. "Those are fairy cakes. That's fairy bread. And that stuff is fairy floss," she said.

Elly peered closely at this last plate. "Fairy floss?" she said. "That's what we use to clean our teeth!"

Caitlin's mom had obviously spent a lot of time on the food. The fairy bread was cut into tiny stars, and the fairy cakes were decorated with hundreds of miniature sugar flowers. Elly and Jess chose a cake each and the sugar flowers dissolved on their tongues.

"Come on," said Jess. "Let's go and join the others. I can't wait to see what their flying inventions are like."

The Fairy Club girls were standing in a group in the corner of the yard. They had a strange-looking object on the ground in front of them—a teapot, with a pair of feathery wings stuck on each side, and a propeller sticking out through the spout.

"This is my latest invention," explained Caitlin. "I've been working on it for weeks."

Elly and Jess looked at the teapot, which was feebly hopping across the lawn. Jess gently picked the teapot up and lifted off the lid. Inside, was a small engine, whirring away.

"What kind of crankshaft are you using?" she asked Caitlin.

"Just a standard one," replied Caitlin. "But I think the problem is the piston rig."

Jess nodded. "I think you're right. And

what might help is—" but before she could finish explaining, something zoomed past her at a very rapid pace.

Unfortunately, Elly's Worry Watch had seen it, too. "WATCH OUT!" it shrieked, as the whirring noise got louder.

Elly looked around. *What was that?*

"I said, 'WATCH OUT!'" screamed the watch again. This time, impatient that Elly wasn't moving, it fired up a tiny jet engine in its base and yanked Elly out of the way. Jess grabbed onto Elly's leg as she was pulled sideways. But the watch's engine was powerful enough to pull both of them up into the air before depositing them right on top of the food table.

All was silent as the Fairy Club girls gaped at the scene before them. It was the sort of silence that you can't ever imagine being

broken. But then the whirring noise started up again, and a moment later, the Hover Lamp landed in Jess's lap, blinking its lights happily.

Chapter Ten

Elly could see stars before her eyes, and she wondered if she had hit her head. Then she realized that the stars she could see were fairy bread stars stuck all over her body. She looked across at Jess. Normally, she would've burst out laughing at the blob of fairy floss on her friend's head—it looked like a sticky pink wig.

But she didn't feel like laughing right now. They had managed to wreck all the

food. They'd probably never get invited to a Fairy Club party again, and they would never get to finish their detective work. Elly got up and peeled off the fairy bread sticking to her arms. This was no time to sit around covered in party food. She hoisted Jess to her feet. Jess tucked the Hover Lamp under her arm.

"Don't worry," Elly announced. "Jess and I will fix everything. Just give us half an hour."

Then she and Jess dashed out of the garden and leaped onto Elly's waiting skateboard.

They stopped at a park around the corner.

"What should we do?" said Jess. "We've got to go back and fix that mess."

Elly looked at her curiously. "I thought you said Fairy Club was dumb," she said.

Jess blushed. "It's different now I know what they really do," she said. "Anyway, we

haven't found out who the fairy is yet."

Elly thought for a moment. "There's only one thing we can do," she said. "We have to make a whole lot of food."

Jess stared at Elly. "What are you talking about?" she said. "There's no way we can remake all that stuff."

Elly smiled. "You've forgotten about our secret weapon," she said. "The Wunch Box!" And she pulled it out of her backpack.

Jess wasn't sure about this idea. But Elly was busy searching through her backpack and, a moment later, triumphantly held something in the air.

"The Wunch Box comes with different dials," explained Elly. "You can swap them around for different situations. This is the party food dial."

She handed it over to Jess. Sure enough, instead of sandwiches and fruit, this dial had such options as party pies and chocolate brownies.

"I'll make party pies first," said Elly, attaching the new dial.

A few minutes later, she opened up the

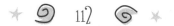

box and it was filled with steaming little pies. They even had a little heart-shaped dollop of cream on the top. The girls loaded them on to a plate that Elly found in her backpack. Jess was starting to understand why Elly always took her backpack with her. She had lots of very useful things stashed away in its little pockets and compartments.

"And now I'll make Jell-O," Elly said, changing the setting on the dial.

The Jell-O was much quicker to make, and less than a minute later, Jess carefully tipped it into a large bowl that appeared from a small side pocket of the backpack. The Jell-O was green with chocolate frogs set into it. There were chocolate tadpoles, too, which Jess had never seen before.

Jess started to feel better. Maybe Elly's

plan was going to work after all.

Elly changed the dial again. "Now, I'll do brownies," she said. She patted the side of the box. "I hope the Wunch Box can manage all this work."

A moment later, steam began to emerge from the box, along with a delicious chocolatey aroma.

"They smell OK, at any rate," said Jess.

But seconds later, the Wunch Box started making huffing noises. It sounded like someone running up a hill. Even worse, the brownies started to smell very strange.

"We'd better check what's going on," said Jess, in alarm.

The noise of the box was getting louder and more agitated. The Hover Lamp was now hiding beneath the layers of Jess's skirt, rattling in fear. Elly opened the box. Inside were several rows of perfect-looking brownies, each with a tiny pair of chocolate wings placed on top.

Elly was relieved. "See?" she said confi-

dently. "Nothing to worry about." She picked up a brownie and took a bite. But almost immediately, she spat it out and made a face. "Gross!" she said.

Nervously, Jess picked one up and took a bite. It definitely didn't taste like a brownie. Yet the flavor was very familiar.

Then it dawned on Jess. "Baked beans!" she exclaimed. "This brownie tastes like baked beans!"

"Oh, no," said Elly in dismay. "That means . . ." She picked up a pie and took a bite. "Lemonade!" she said, screwing up her face.

Jess tasted the Jell-O. "Corn chips!" she said. She couldn't help laughing. "It's so weird. It tastes exactly like them. It'd be cool except—"

"Except that no one wants to eat corn chip-flavored Jell-O," finished Elly, bitterly.

 116

"Especially not at a party."

Jess had to agree. "No. The flavors are getting muddled somehow," she said. She picked up the box. It was probably something pretty simple. If she had enough time, she might even be able to fix it. But there was no time left.

"What are we going to do now?" wailed Elly so loudly that the Hover Lamp began blinking its lights in distress.

Jess didn't know what to say. It looked like a hopeless situation.

Suddenly, there was a voice behind them. "Perhaps I could be of assistance?"

Elly and Jess turned around. It was Ms. Buttercup. "Ms. Buttercup!" said Elly, in surprise. "What are *you* doing here?"

It was *very* weird the way Ms. Buttercup

always seemed to turn up just when things were going horribly wrong.

"Well, Elly," said Ms. Buttercup, smiling. "I'm your human godmother, and I'm here to give you a hand."

Chapter Eleven

Elly and Jess stared at Ms. Buttercup with their mouths wide open. Thousands of thoughts rushed through their minds and got tangled trying to escape from their mouths.

But Ms. Buttercup seemed to already know what they wanted to know. "Yes," she said to Elly, "I know you're a fairy. I've known for a long time, in fact." Then she looked at Jess. "And yes, I know that you know Elly's secret identity."

Jess and Elly looked at her in alarm. This was bad news. If the Fairydom authorities found out, Elly would be in big trouble.

"No need to fret," Ms. Buttercup assured them. "I won't tell a soul. My job is to make life easier for you, Elly, not more difficult! And besides," she added, "Jess is exactly the sort of friend a fairy like you needs."

Elly breathed a sigh of relief. But then she suddenly felt a bit annoyed. "Why haven't I seen you before, then?" she asked. There had been *lots* of times when she could've used a human godmother.

"Sorry about that. I have loads of fairy goddaughters," she said, "and sometimes I lose track of them all."

"Are you a fairy, Ms. Buttercup?" asked Jess.

Ms. Buttercup shook her head. "No,

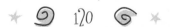

I'm a human. You see, humans have fairy godmothers," she explained. "And fairies have human godmothers. I'm Elly's."

Elly was puzzled. "If you're not a fairy, then how did you do all that magic?" she asked, suspiciously. "The basketball and the sausage rolls?"

Ms. Buttercup tapped her hand on the big black handbag she wore over her shoulder. "This is my human godmother kit," explained Ms. Buttercup. "It contains lots of useful gadgets. Most human godmothers hardly ever have to use their kits, but I've used mine a lot looking after Elly."

She opened up her handbag and the girls peered inside. Jess was disappointed. "It looks just like my mom's bag," she said.

Ms. Buttercup smiled. "That's exactly how

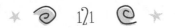

it's supposed to look. All the gadgets are disguised." She pulled out a tube of lip gloss. "This, for instance, is how I stopped the sausage rolls rolling. It's Gravity Gel. I dabbed a little on the bottom of the tray and it added just enough force to keep those rolls weighed down."

Jess examined the lip gloss carefully. It looked so ordinary that she wasn't sure if she believed Ms. Buttercup.

"What would happen if you accidentally put some on your lips?" she asked curiously.

Ms. Buttercup frowned. "Oh, you wouldn't want to do that," she said. "Your lips would end up dragging on the ground."

"What about the basketball?" asked Elly. "How did you make it act that way?"

Ms. Buttercup produced a small flashlight.

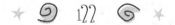

122

HUMAN GODMOTHER KIT

invisible mending tape

handkerchief spell warmer

perfume smell-a-scope

extra-tricky lip gloss (disguised)

it looks like a flashlight, but is it?

kooky, crazy keys

very sneaky purse

"With this," she said, handing it to Jess. "It is an Unpredict-a-Ball guiding light. The ball follows the flashlight beam."

Jess turned on the flashlight. "I can't see anything," she protested.

"Of course not!" Ms. Buttercup laughed. "Have you heard of a dog whistle?"

Jess nodded. "It's a whistle that's so high-pitched, humans can't hear it, but dogs can," she said.

"Exactly," agreed Ms. Buttercup. "Well, this flashlight is like that. It has a light so bright that humans can't see it. But objects—like basketballs and tennis balls—are drawn to it like a magnet."

"But why did you want me to do so well at basketball?" asked Elly.

Ms. Buttercup shrugged. "I was sick of

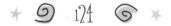

watching Clarabelle win. She cheats, you know?"

But Ms. Buttercup looked a bit puzzled as she put the flashlight back in her bag. She looked like she was deciding whether or not to say something. "It's strange, though," she whispered, looking over her shoulder to check that no one was listening. "The Unpredict-a-Ball batteries ran out halfway through the game!"

"You mean . . . ?" began Jess.

"I knew it!" squealed Elly. "I *knew* there was another fairy at the school."

"Well," said Ms. Buttercup, "I can't be sure, but I have been wondering for a while now."

Suddenly, Jess remembered the party and the ruined food. "Have you got any other cool things in there?" asked Jess, hopefully.

"I've got this!" said Ms. Buttercup, pulling

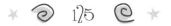

out a large white hanky. Then, to Jess and Elly's surprise, she spat on it and started wiping vigorously at Elly's cheeks.

Elly didn't like it very much. It was the sort of thing her aunties did when they visited. "What magic does *that* do?" she asked, doubtfully.

"Oh, it's not magic," replied Ms. Buttercup. "You just had some fairy bread stuck to your face. It's incredible what you can do with a wet hanky!"

Elly checked the time on her Worry Watch. If they were away for much longer, the party would be over. "Ms. Buttercup, have you got anything that will help fix this mess we're in?" she asked.

She couldn't see how a flashlight or some lip gloss was going to remake a whole lot of

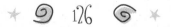

party food. She just hoped that somewhere in that enormous bag, there were several large plates of fairy bread.

Ms. Buttercup pulled something out from deep in her bag and handed it to Elly.

Jess stared at it in surprise. "Tape?" she asked. "Are you suggesting we use tape to fix all that food?"

But Elly knew what it was. And that was when she knew that Ms. Buttercup really was her human godmother. "It's invisible mending tape," she explained to Jess excitedly. "It's the coolest stuff."

She picked up one of the baked bean-flavored brownies and broke it in half. "Watch this," she said. She tore off a piece of tape and placed it carefully on one half of the brownie. Immediately, the other half zoomed

127

across the ground to meet it, until the two halves were joined back together again.

Jess picked up the brownie. "Amazing," she said, peeling off the tape. "You'd never know it had been broken."

"It's very useful," said Ms. Buttercup. "I find it handy for locating missing socks." Then she produced something else from the cavernous bag. It looked like an ordinary perfume bottle, but Jess had a feeling it would be something else. "This will come in handy," said Ms. Buttercup. "It's a Food Fixer. If you spray any food that's been flattened, the Food Fixer will pump it full of air again."

Elly took the bottle and the tape and put them in her backpack. "Thanks, Ms. Buttercup," she said, gratefully. It was still going to be difficult to fix up all that food, but it would be much easier with these gadgets.

"That's quite all right, Elly," said Ms. Buttercup. "That's what I'm here for, after all." Then she looked at Elly's face closely, and before Elly knew what was happening, Ms. Buttercup had pulled out her hanky again. "I can still see a couple of dirty spots, Elly," she said, leaning close. "Let me clean you up before you go—"

But Elly grabbed Jess's arm and together they ran off hastily down the street. "Thanks again, Ms. Buttercup!" called Elly over her shoulder.

Back at the party, the guests seemed to

have forgotten all about the food anyway. They were still trying to get the teapot to fly.

"Let's fix up the food while they're not watching," whispered Elly. "And before Caitlin's mom comes out and sees what a mess we've made."

So, the two girls quickly got to work repairing the food. Jess used the invisible mending tape while Elly pumped up the flattened food. Jess found it fascinating. Adding tape to the tiniest cake crumb caused hundreds of other cake crumbs to come flying from wherever they had scattered. One large crumb was even whisked away from the beak of a very surprised bird.

It wasn't long before the food table was looking almost exactly as it had before. It was in the nick of time, too, for just as they finished, the teapot came hopping across the lawn, flapping its wings madly. The Hover Lamp, which had been sitting on Jess's shoulder while she worked, made a growling noise when it saw the teapot, and started to swoop toward it. Luckily Jess grabbed it before it could do any more damage.

The Fairy Club girls stared in disbelief at the table. They walked around it, touching things.

Caitlin had a funny little half smile on her face. "How did you do that?" she asked Elly and Jess. "It looks exactly like it did before." She raised one eyebrow.

Elly smiled modestly. "Oh, it was nothing," she said, looking at Caitlin's small feet.

Jess did a quick freckle count. Caitlin had nine perfect little freckles.

chapter twelve

Y ou don't need to hear about the rest of the party—except, perhaps, to hear that it was a great success. But you might like to know that a number of unexpected and extraordinary things occurred in the short time that was left. The first extraordinary thing was that Caitlin and Jess managed to get the teapot to glide in a straight line for ten yards, before crashing into the fence.

The next extraordinary thing was that

after Clarabelle saw the teapot flying, she actually smiled. Then she, Caitlin, and Jess spent the rest of the party deep in conversation about pistons and cogs. The final extraordinary thing was that when Elly and Jess left the party, they both had pink Fairy Club badges pinned to their outfits. And they both looked very happy about it, which was perhaps the most extraordinary—and unexpected—thing of all.

Elly and Jess had the badges pinned to their sweaters on Monday morning as they got ready for school. Elly caught Jess staring at it proudly.

"I never thought I'd see you so happy to be a member of Fairy Club," teased Elly.

Jess looked embarrassed. "It's more of an invention club, really," she said, as they climbed on their bikes. "What Caitlin doesn't know about cogs isn't worth knowing."

But when they arrived at school, there were a number of shocks waiting for them. The first happened when they walked into their classroom, where instead of seeing Ms. Buttercup's smiling face, they saw Mrs. Snidely's scowling one.

"Where's Ms. Buttercup?" asked Elly, in surprise.

"She's been called away on an urgent matter," said Mrs. Snidely. "Something to do with one of her goddaughters, apparently. I will be teaching you for the next few weeks."

Then a moment later, an announcement came over the loudspeaker. It was Mrs. Hayman, the principal. "Elly Knottleweed-Eversprightly, please come to my office."

Elly looked at Jess in alarm. She recognized a certain tone in Mrs. Hayman's voice. It was the Tone of Trouble. *But what could it possibly be about?* For once, she hadn't caused any trouble at school and, with the help of Ms. Buttercup, had actually done very well.

Elly went straight to the principal's office. Mrs. Hayman had a very strange look on her

face. It was like she'd just been given the biggest chocolate cake in the world. "Take a seat, Elly," said Mrs. Hayman, smiling. "You have a visitor. And such a delightful one! What a lucky girl you are."

Elly looked at the principal suspiciously. *What was going on?*

"Hello, Elinora," said a familiar voice.

Elly spun around. Standing behind her was Grandmother Knottleweed-Eversprightly. She was wearing a shimmering silver and mauve coat and a very disapproving expression. Elly recognized the coat right away. It was a Charming Coat, which made humans think that the wearer was the most delightful person they'd ever met, no matter how rude the wearer was actually being. It also wiped humans' memories after the conversation.

 136

Grandmother Knottleweed-Eversprightly wore hers whenever she met a human because she tended to be very, very rude—and she couldn't be bothered being secretive.

Grandmother Knottleweed-Eversprightly moved across the room like clouds move across the sky before it starts raining. Somehow, she managed to look both light and heavy at the same time.

"What a magnificent person your grandmother is!" gushed Mrs. Hayman. "Such style, such grace."

"Oh, do be quiet," snapped Grandmother Knottleweed-Eversprightly.

But instead of being offended, Mrs. Hayman laughed. "And so amusing, too!" she said.

"I just returned from my book tour last night," Grandmother Knottleweed-Eversprightly said, ignoring Mrs. Hayman, who was staring at her admiringly. "Only to discover the dreadful mistake your parents had made! Why they decided to let you go on an undercover operation in this terrible school, I have no idea."

Mrs. Hayman blushed. "You're too kind," she said. "It is a dreadful school, isn't it?"

Elly was angry. "It's not dreadful at all. It's a great school and I want to stay here. I'm doing really well and I'm learning all about humans. I'm even on the basketball team."

But her grandmother already had her by the arm. "That's impossible," she replied. "You need to go to a proper fairy school where you'll learn much more important things than basketball."

"So true, so true!" chortled Mrs. Hayman.

"Your grandmother is a very wise woman, Elly."

Grandmother Knottleweed-Eversprightly would've whisked Elly away right then and there, but Elly managed to persuade her to give her time to collect her things. It was recess, and Elly found Jess deep in conversation with Caitlin and Clarabelle about flying machines.

Elly pulled Jess over to a quiet corner of the playground and explained the situation.

"You can't go," said Jess, sadly. "School has just started getting good now that you're here."

Elly sighed. "There's no saying 'no' to Grandmother Knottleweed-Eversprightly," she said, gloomily.

The Hover Lamp was sitting in its usual place on Jess's shoulder. It had hardly left Jess's side since they met. Jess passed it to Elly.

"You'd better take this, I guess," she said.

Elly held the lamp for a moment. The lamp began making a noise that was so much like howling that she quickly handed it back to Jess. "I think you'd better keep it," she said. "It seems very attached to you."

The Hover Lamp seemed relieved to be back with Jess. It made a happy, purring sort of sound.

Elly looked down at her wrist and sighed. "I just wish this Worry Watch was a little less attached to me."

As she spoke, the Worry Watch suddenly unbuckled itself and dropped to the ground. The girls stared at it in surprise.

"It must have decided that Grandmother Knottleweed-Eversprightly will do enough worrying for all of us," sighed Elly.

Jess bent down and carefully picked the watch up. She turned it over. "Look!" she said. "There's another setting on the back."

Sure enough, there was a little red arrow pointing to the word WORRY. But below it was another word: RELAX. Jess flicked the switch over with her thumb. The watch immediately began swinging its arms around in a very careless fashion as if it really didn't care what the time was.

"Don't hurry, don't worry," it said, in a soothing, sleepy voice. "Everything is going to be fine."

Elly grinned. "For once, I think this watch might just be right," she said, giving Jess a big hug.

GOFISH

MEREDITH BADGER

What did you want to be when you grew up?
The first thing I ever wanted to be was a tightrope walker because I liked the idea of wearing a pink tutu and holding onto a parasol. My balance isn't very good though, so I soon realized it wasn't the best career choice for me.

When did you realize you wanted to be a writer?
Pretty much as soon as I got over the whole tightrope walking thing I decided that being a children's writer and illustrator was what I wanted to be. I used to make books with my dad when I was around four. I'd draw the pictures and tell him what to write on each page.

What's your first childhood memory?
I remember my third birthday party. One of the guests (a little boy) tried to tell me that it was actually his party, not mine. I remember thinking "but isn't it a bit weird that my parents would throw a party for someone else?"

SQUARE FISH

What's your most embarrassing childhood memory?
Walking into the wrong toilet block at school—the boys' block instead of the girls'.

What's your favorite childhood memory?
Going on camping holidays with my cousins over summer

As a young person, who did you look up to most?
I really admired anyone who wrote books. I wrote fan letters to authors I liked and it was so exciting if they wrote back. My dad wrote a nonfiction book when I was in primary school and I was so proud I nearly burst. I took the book to show-and-tell to brag about him to my friends.

What was your worst subject in school?
I was really terrible at math and sports.

What was your best subject in school?
English!

What was your first job?
I had a holiday job working in a shopping center. My duties included collecting up the money from the public phones and making announcements over the PA to say things like "Mr. Brown, your wife is waiting for you by the donut shop. Please return there immediately."

Where do you write your books?
I work anywhere—anywhere except a proper office for some reason. I often work at the kitchen table and recently I've been doing a lot of work at the library. So long as I have my laptop with me, I'm fine!

Where do you find inspiration for your writing?
Some of my ideas come from real life things that happened to me or my friends. For instance, in one of my books the main character accidentally walks into the wrong toilet block at school. I also get ideas from eavesdropping on people, especially in the park when I take my daughter there.

Which of your characters is most like you?
I think all my characters are like me a little bit—just different aspects of me. The one I'd most like to be like is Elly from *Fairy School Dropout* because she can fly (even though she doesn't really like it) and because she has a mum who invents lots of great gadgets. I'd also like to be Poppy from *Tweenie Genie* because she has a genie bottle of her own that she can slide into.

When you finish a book, who reads it first?
Sometimes my partner, Matt, reads it first, but usually it's one of my editors.

Are you a morning person or a night owl?
Hmmm . . . I think I like lunchtime best!

What's your idea of the best meal ever?
Sushi to start then maybe a slice of apple strudel for dessert. That's a pretty weird combination though, isn't it?

Which do you like better: cats or dogs?
Cats

What do you value most in your friends?
The ability to make me feel happy when I'm sad

Where do you go for peace and quiet?
To sleep. I have a young daughter, so generally things are pretty noisy wherever we go.

What makes you laugh out loud?
People being silly when I'm not expecting it

Who is your favorite fictional character?
I love the three Fossil sisters in *Ballet Shoes*—Pauline, Petrova, and Posy. I wanted to be all three of them when I was growing up.

What time of year do you like best?
The first weeks of autumn when it's not too hot and not too cold

If you were stranded on a desert island, who would you want for company?
Someone with a boat maybe?

If you could travel in time, where would you go?
I'd love to see a real dinosaur, but I'd want to make sure that the dinosaur couldn't see me before I time-traveled back there.

What's the best advice you have ever received about writing?
"I think you'd better rewrite this part." It hurts to hear it, but whenever an editor tells me that, it always ends up improving the book.

 SQUARE FISH

What would you do if you ever stopped writing?
I've often thought I'd love to be a jeweler, except that I'd worry all the time about losing the gemstones. Maybe a teacher.

What is your worst habit?
Forgetting to close the fridge properly

What do you wish you could do better?
I'm a hopeless cook—I really wish I were better at that. Also math. It's pretty useful.

Elly is no fan of being a fairy, and she's been a
failure at every fairy school she's attended.
Now she's stuck at a fairy *boarding* school,
with no hope for escape.

Will this be Elly's biggest disaster ever, or could
she finally become a proper fairy? Find out in

Fairy School Dropout: Over the Rainbow

chapter One

Imagine this: You are walking through a park and you see a girl and an old lady hurrying along. The girl looks like a normal, average schoolgirl, except her feet are slightly on the small side and her hair is very, very shiny. Perhaps you decide that the old lady is the girl's grandmother. She looks like she's probably saying, "Come along, dear. Let's get home so your old gran can make you a batch of cookies."

You smile, thinking, *What a lovely granny, and what a typical, ordinary girl. They must be going on a stroll together—the sort we humans go on all the time.*

Well, you're right about one thing—the old lady is the girl's grandmother. But everything else you thought was wrong. Totally, utterly wrong. For a start, there's nothing typical or ordinary about the girl. She's a fairy, and her name is Elly.

Her grandmother is a fairy, too. But Elly's grandmother isn't exactly lovely.

What she was actually saying to Elly as they hurried through the park was, "I don't know what your parents were thinking, sending you to a human school while they are away. It's not as if you didn't already have some very bad habits! I've left a message for

your mother, telling her that I'm taking you to a *proper* fairy school. A good, strict one with no humans!"

Grandmother led Elly toward the center of the local gardens. For such a tiny lady, she had a very tight grip.

"Um, excuse me, Grandmother," said Elly in her politest voice.

"What, Elinora?" snapped Grandmother.

"It's just that I know there aren't any fairy schools in this park," said Elly.

Grandmother stopped suddenly by the large fountain in the middle of the park. "The school I'm taking you to is not in this *park*," she retorted. "It's in Rainbowville."

Elly looked at her grandmother in surprise. "Rainbowville!" she repeated. Rainbowville was the capital of Fairydom. "I've never been."

3

"Well, it's about time you went," said Grandmother. "Only fairies are allowed in there. It will do you good to be separated from all those ghastly human children."

"They're not ghastly. Most of them are really nice," Elly said crossly. "Much nicer than a lot of fairies I know," she added under her breath. "Like Gabi Cruddleperry, for instance."

Gabilotta Cruddleperry had been at Elly's last fairy school—Mossy Blossom Academy. She and Elly had been enemies ever since Elly had accidentally given her a big moustache on their first day at school. Gabi had been trying to get even with Elly ever since.

"What?" asked Grandmother sharply.

"Nothing!" Elly replied hastily. "I was just wondering—how do we get to Rainbowville?"

Grandmother looked annoyed. "Over the

rainbow, of course!" she said. "You should know all about the Rainbow Portal from reading the Fairy Code."

Elly kept quiet. The Fairy Code was a huge rule book that school fairies were supposed to read every day. Whenever Elly tried to read it, however, she fell asleep! But there was no way she could tell Grandmother that. Especially as some Knottleweed-Eversprightly ancestor had helped write it.

"We need to catch ourselves a rainbow," said Grandmother, producing a large, multi-colored umbrella from somewhere in her coat.

Elly looked up at the clear blue sky. "I don't think it's going to rain," she said doubtfully. "And besides, just as you get close to a rainbow, it vanishes!"

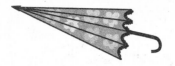

Grandmother unfurled the umbrella. "It's not a matter of finding the end of the rainbow," she explained condescendingly. "It's about getting the rainbow to come to you."

Elly had to try very hard not to giggle. Everyone knew that rainbows didn't come to you when you called!

But then Grandmother held the umbrella up and the most extraordinary thing happened. Droplets of water began rising out of the fountain and floating toward the umbrella. Before long, a fine mist hung in the air. Then a rainbow appeared in the center of the mist, arching up into the sky.

"Wow!" gasped Elly.

The rainbow was very bright, and the colors seemed to pulse and shimmer. As Elly watched, the rainbow grew bigger and stronger, stretching up into the sky.

"Come here," instructed Grandmother. She grabbed Elly and jumped onto the rainbow.

Then Elly found herself hurtling up the rainbow. *I feel like I'm on a giant roller coaster,* giggled Elly to herself, as she whooshed higher and higher. *I wish I could do this on my skateboard!*

The rainbow was smooth and slightly spongy to sit on, but completely dry. Elly gripped the rainbow's sides to steady herself.

Down below, the town got smaller and smaller until Elly could hardly see it at all.

With a little bounce, Elly and her grandmother arrived at the top of the rainbow. Looking down, Elly saw something amazing.

 7

On one side of the rainbow was the town she'd grown up in. And on the other side was a vast, magical-looking city, twinkling and gleaming in the sunlight.

Rainbowville! thought Elly excitedly.

"Hold on very tight, Elinora!" called Grandmother as they began zooming down the other side. "We're almost there."

 8